SKY GODS
and CHAOS MONSTERS

SKY GODS
and CHAOS MONSTERS

Glen M. Graham

RESOURCE *Publications* · Eugene, Oregon

SKY GODS AND CHAOS MONSTERS

Resource Publications
An Imprint of Wipf and Stock Publishers
199 W. 8th Ave., Suite 3
Eugene, OR 97401

www.wipfandstock.com

PAPERBACK ISBN: 979-8-3852-5313-5
HARDCOVER ISBN: 979-8-3852-5314-2
EBOOK ISBN: 979-8-3852-5315-9

VERSION NUMBER 072925

For Ellie

Contents

Chapter 1
Dawn

in sleep again
amniotic currents brush against your ears
the swaying dance repeated
the heartbeat counting out the rhythms
inside my chest
you cower
between my ribs
entangled in arteries and veins
the unbroken surface of our bodies
endless
do not forget
this sleep
child
do not breathe yet
before this journey is done
before the time of individual hearts
do not open your eyes

I see you before I awake
crouched by the fire
you break shells
dry acorns in the sun
you pound them in the stone mortar

then fill the willow twig filters
with mash and water
again and again
first hot
then cold
until the bitters extract

under your feet
the earth shifts
a bird song
escapes
spins
scatters in the air
I abandon every note
I discard the hovel home
you erect it again
collect every sound
call every spirit
in your careless care
Mother
loving Mother
shameless Mother
you draw water among the tule reeds
at las Temblores
pick seeds and berries
under the willows and cottonwoods
your frail nostrils
feral eyes
alert to any scent
any flickering shadow
your feet are heavy
tied to the soil
innocent
wading
mulling about in the water
you are a useless dream

Dawn

a vanishing scent
I have not come to touch your face
or sit at your feet
only to crowd the dark corners
the empty spaces
to catch a glimpse
if possible
like all strangers
to gawk
heartless
like all strangers
to return home again
victorious
your artless fables
your Indian charms stuffed in pocket
all of this was yours
Mother
it was never yours

between the willows and the cottonwoods
a pregnant hare flees
beyond this land to another
a crow beats the air
ignorant of the cruelty to come
lift your head
Mother
dumb bird
flee your nest
cower in fear
fearless children
there are men who cannot dream
who defy the seasons
who turn stone to dust
they clear the woods and level the hills
through the valley
the beast-slayers on horseback

Portolà and his men
a leather-jacketed procession
legs and arms diseased
skin flecked with lesions
ships half-destroyed
look Mother
on the horizon
a light stalks the hills
the day of vengeance is here
burn your hovels
purify the stench
there is no time for bitterness
the Great Mystery has passed
all is gone
every single blueberry bush and cottonwood
every single acorn tree
beyond Las Temblores to the hills
it was all yours
it was never yours
you are now beggars in a land of plenty

       you are still a child
       I still know your name
       the name before all names

       on the sixth day
       on the day of your naming
       the elders dug a hole in the centre of the hut
       they kindled the fire
       heated the stones until red hot
       they covered them with wild tansy and earth
       I took you in my arms
       wrapped you in a mat
       straddled the embers
       water poured into the opening
       steam surged upward

4

Dawn

so hot it burned my skin
so hot I skipped and danced
stainless
we lay on the earth
covered in blankets
sweating
waiting for food
inside the coiled wrap
you struggled
you stretched your arms
ripped your swaddling clothes
you walked into sunlight
and began to dance in circles
faster and faster
until your roots grew deep into the ground
fed by streams far below
you reached for the sky
the birds built nests on your branches
and the wild animals found rest in your shade
at dusk you fell to ground
sank into the soil
into my arms
we lay in the blanket
we fell asleep together
until dawn
my child you are still my son
I still know your name
the name before all names
do not turn from me
do not hide your face
do not breathe yet
before this journey is done
before the time of individual hearts
do not open your eyes

on the shore

the gods slay the beast
they find her body in the sand gasping for air
they pierce her heart with a spear
carry the corpse over the hills
through the valley
Portolà dismounts
a breeze kicks up
twirls light and shade
tips of grass sparkle in the sun
he dips his feet in the river
the water cools his skin
heals his sores
he strolls among the wild grapevines and asparagus
takes rest between the willows and sycamores
the villagers return with their tule rafts
baskets filled with tuna and mussel

> *look at these fields*
> *these rivers*
> *these woods*
> *this is paradise*
> *the food*
> *it nearly detaches itself and falls into our open hands*

that evening
on the darkest of nights
Portolà drinks a dismal drink
an awful spirit cuts his throat
sets his blood on fire
near the edge of camp
in the shadows
out of reach
his body sways
falls
crumbles in the leaves under the alders
then a shameful
beastly sleep
during the night

he cuts himself on a thorn
the blood stains his leg
leaks into the soil
the hollow bone
infused
the vigilant mind
scattered
a deer approaches in the moonlight
it breathes into Portolà's nostrils
he takes his first breath
awakens
before the first strand of light
before a single word is spoken
he collects the remains
cuts the roots
washes his body

I find a fossil on the bank
dead veins
ancient blood trails
announce the passing of some insect
moments before flight
I skip the stone on the water
it hits three times
then sinks to the bottom
I go to Portolà and rescue him
I let him cover my skin
comb my hair
collect my heathen limbs

> *give me a new name*
> *Portolà*
> *breathe on me*
> *lead me*
> *and I will follow*
> *there is fresh water and arable land to sow*
> *I will open my eyes*

I will cast all this aside
lead me
speak
and I will listen

in the shadows among the cottonwoods
a dragon fly lifts his legs
takes flight into the sunlight
the voices beckon
a flickering light
a scent in the breeze
the mist evaporates

child
wake up now
from this dream

the membrane of sleep trembles

a breeze too weak shifts in the ceiling

the smell of human excrement
in my nostrils

the source of the smell
an improvised latrine in the center of the monjerio

through a single window near the ceiling
I hear the toll of instruments in soil
the work areas rousing with men

through hides strung out like crosses
tannery tanks
tallow vats for candles and soap
our field men scatter to the harvest

the soil bleeds insects

Dawn

the machine beats blood
impelled by some unknown mechanism
bone sinks on bone
muscles grow to size
the huts of the newly planted we built stand silent

I take Portolà's hand
we walk from the monjero
through a crowd of workers
we cross the field to the chapel
enter the darkness
the baptistery
its hammered copper font
sparkles in my eyes
the candles dance in the breeze
we lay the beast on the alter
Portolà cuts me open
draws me into the light
I arch my head back
above me beams of oak trees
the food of Tongva
pulled from the ground
here the frame
the hidden skeleton
the branches we slit
the stroke ingrained in the heart of trees
I cannot gaze for long
these thoughts have no place
the surface is cold
the roots dig in vain

> *you are Prospero*
> *I am Prospero*

rehearse the lines
with me

> *I baptize you in the name of the Father*

you are El Rio de Nuestra Senora la Reina de Los Angeles
you are El Pueblo de Los Angeles

        before the day of your naming
        before time of croaking frogs
        we took ax to pine
        cut the Kotoomut pole
        we hung our mortuary baskets on the branches
        we danced
        we remembered dead
        collected all the stories
        called all the spirits
now foiled by worms
the poll sinks to ground
the soil collects every memory
your father's father
your mother's mother
the father of all
the mother of all
all have passed
muscles lock in place
steps measure time
all is hope
all is destiny
all is future tense
Mother pay no attention to those who still remember
those who cannot rejoice
those who falter
stumble across the syllables
misspeak the names
when the moon is dark they run the woods
they escape on unknown paths
cower in distant fields
the dogs find them floundering on footpaths
the soldiers return them to the mission
shackle them

brand them
free them
attach the legs
insert the eyes
repeat the lessons from scratch
again and again
pay no attention Mother
they never learned
it is a muscle to strengthen
a motion to repeat
the child who sleeps silently
awakens to the sound of footsteps outside
the voices of men through a crack in the doorway
they beckon with trinkets
soon the child joins them
this happens with time
with time the lesson takes root
Mother I am a wild space
hungering for a name
I am a prophesy in the wilderness
I am a suckling child thirsting for blood
I am skin untouched sleeping at dawn
begging for the heavy weight
forgive me mother
forgive me savage child
the gods cleared the path
they slayed the beast
now all is empty
the hour looms
the plan unfurls
great void
Great Mystery
write your name on my forehead
I have not called on you since Mother
I have not worn you on the inside
I have swallowed and all is gone

sweet Mother
I am merciless now

> my child
> you still know how to burn the brush hovels
> how to move on
> what will you do with these adobe houses
> you who cannot purify them
> they remain steadfast
> they do not pass with the season
> with the rising river
> the scent of disease hangs in every corner
> you still know the names of these rivers
> you still know your name
> the name before all other names
> before the time of croaking frogs
> you still remember how to hunt with the
> makana
> you still remember the blueberry bushes and
> tule reeds
> every single cottonwood
> acorn tree
> beyond Las Temblores to the hills
> my child
> do not fear
> I want to see your hand
> your soft skin
> your scared skin
> we will eat together by the fire
> a story will pass of other places
> strange habits and fearsome gods
> will you remain silent
> will you turn your face from me forever
> do not turn from me
> do not hide
> do not breathe yet

Dawn

before this journey is done
before the time of individual hearts
do not open your eyes

history must proceed
dust blow hard
along the north wall of the church
where the cemetery holds a hundred gravestones
there is evidence
wooden monuments
illegible honor to the lives of various missionaries
the mission is silent
the stonewalls divulge nothing
the grapevines are thick with age
in the middle a large wooden cross to remember
6,000 Indians buried in unmarked graves
Prospero's great-great granddaughter
sits below a goldfish bowl and old photos
census records
marriage books
copied mission registries fill the cabinets
she tells of how Prospero survived
married a Spanish soldier's daughter and built a home by a creek
and a hollow of sycamores
I need to pass this on to someone or another chapter will be lost
she says
she tells of how syphilis consumed the blood of young men
of how the women found work as streetwalkers
she tells of Indians set adrift when the mission was disbanded
of men who found jobs with the Spanish and the English
some of them compensated for their work with alcohol
then arrested for drunkenness
then auctioned off as indentured servants at the pueblo Los An-
geles corral
she tells of how the Anglos invading from the East
drove the Tongva from the fisheries and acorn groves

muddied the rivers and creeks
destroying food supplies everywhere
a hundred Indian affairs in all

muted conversations rise in the sun
visitors walk softly in the courtyard
afraid to stir the dead
a stone marker in memory of the Old Mission
failing inscriptions tell of fruit orchards
decked with orange and yellow valencia
cuttings from mother vines
cattle and sheep roam in unfenced fields
beneath the courtyard it is obvious
how our city follows the trails of ancient tribes
follows the course the rivers took
how ranchos reoccupied the desolated sites
boom towns replacing the ranchos
grids filling in the open spaces
melded to adjacent grids
the site of Yangna is downtown
Tsavingna is San Pedro
Engnovagna Redondo
the trails from village to village freeways
Suangna is an Ugly Duckling used-car lot
traffic beside an oil refinery
an empty field
neo-Nazi graffiti on a storm drain

past endless fields
pipelines cross the hillsides and riverbanks
steal arms mine the earth
down to Cesar Chavez
the journey continues
solely attentive to dead-ends
cul de sacs
I eat maps

plot turns and intersections
the city unfurls
a tourist book takes me from Boyle Heights to the Pacific Ocean
Cesar Chavez is a journal entry
San Gabriel is captioned in aging brochures
it is not for a stranger to breathe here
or balance guilt and fear
I must know and yet remain ignorant
take gloss of ancient sites
frown at dried up rivers
I must burden relatives back home with crime statistics
become a journalist
with pen in mouth and owlish face
glued to facts and figures
the solemn cell
insulated
against all sound
the elegant turn
the flippant wave
leaves everything untouched
men shaped inside my brain
take the form of gangs
burdened by the crimes of previous days
women cornered by the sunrise
keep their place cold and dense
rooted in some other soil
fed by unknown rivers
there are children here
with poison in their bodies
there are children who smile when I pass
there is lung and spit
breath hot with living
a parking lot trek is measured in heartbeats
the shallow lung
the white eye
the boys on the corner

brown and dangerous
I am neighborless
unseen
only a dull stare
searching the sky
I have nothing to say here
useless talking
soulless sound
I am light in the eyes
a mindless distraction
a spectacle of words
shall I speak or listen
carry on this conversation
continue the monologue
become a thousand voices or none

Mother I have come back one last time
on this last day
before the last day
even now at White Memorial
the nameless shape of white-coated men steal past
outside your hospice room
their angular faces
heavy-footed and laborious
should their feet lose ground
called to other destinations
they would greet me if time permitted
we'd feel the warmth in each other's hands
the landscape of our skin
but there is nothing here to speak of
they have long since bleached these walls of stain
stripped the artifacts
called off the hunt
I return with pen in pocket to brave your secrets
though the thoughts still bleed out
I was warned of this

Dawn

of a nakedness made necessary with age
even now to my astonishment
it happens
the cells break
the daily insurgence looms
the tentacles sprout again
words purple with love rise in the morning sun
the streets fill up

    thick with people
    on Brooklyn and Soto

    news boys crying out

        hawking papers
        stacks of newspapers on every corner
        the headlines proclaim war
        the prophets warn of retribution
        there are Black folks here and Jews and Mexi-
        cans and Europeans
        we all go to Curry's Ice Cream
        or find our perch at Ginsberg's Vegetarian
        Restaurant
        I watch my dad caught in some conversation
        with his commie friends and union people
        crowds gather on the street sounding their po-
        litical arguments
        their voices resonating off the buildings
        the common breath in our nostrils
        the same air released and drawn
        we are refugees seeking the spoken word
        the word that says you are alive
        born under the same sky
        you who have eyes to see
        hair to comb
        a mouth to kiss

we sleep in each other's homes
eat in each other's kitchens
kids in my block
their parents give me matzas
my mother gives them tortillas
at Christmas the Buddhist priest at the Nichiren
Temple dresses up as Santa Claus and passes out
presents
and we think this is normal
on Sunday the older folks gather by the Hollen-
beck bandstand for their picnic
they eat concletin and we play on the hill
we roll our bodies down towards the stream
at the bottom there's a Japanese bridge
each Sunday it carries us across the river into
magical kingdoms
there are canoes and motorboats for rental
they make our escape from monsters
we twist and turn with river
make our way onto the banks
cover our bodies with foliage and wait it out
there

one Sunday Peter the boy I like flops beside me
the air in his lungs is heavy and grave
we lie next to each other
we breathe together
until we cannot stand the silence
then we build a shelter for ourselves by the river
we dig our fingers into the soil by the bank
Peter finds a shoe and some car part washed up
on shore
he opens his hands
pries her fingers into its corners inside the hol-
low space
he cuts himself and begins to bleed

Dawn

I put his hand into the water
a trail of blood flows with the current

later we take a boat into the water
remove the straight pins in our pockets and
bend them
we attach pieces of bread and some thread and
lower the rods until the minnows appear
one by one we draw them into our boats
hold them up with fanfare
they twist and turn
gasp for air
then fall from our hands and disappear below
the surface

I still remember

before our first kiss
the last Sunday picnic

before the day of vengeance

suddenly a breeze through the valley
strikes against the trees
the light flickers between the leaves
the shadows dance

then darkness

walls of granite

scrape against each other

the earth shakes

   three times in a single day

underneath the currents betray us
deep and wild
black blood boils to the surface
the river bleeds into the streets
around the edges of our feet
into the corners of our conversations
between our teeth
we stumble
shoot the first arrow
pierce the beast
we dam the flow
bring in an army corps

three million barrels of concrete to pave it over

> *I forgot did we not name this river Rio de las Temblores*
> *and this building Mission of the Temblores*
> *how could I forget*
> *these terrestrial convulsions*
> *they were not only monthly and weekly but daily*
> *long ago I complained about the constant blowing of the wind*
> *I said the Indians that did arrive at the mission were blown in by*
> *the four winds*

Mother
it was all a dream
we abandoned it all to the deep
we discarded it all
in your careless care
loving Mother
shameless Mother
wake up
the daughters of darkness are here
one by one
hiding among us
stalking the streets
it could be anyone of us
a Nazi or a Red

our Japanese neighbor
the Mexican on the corner
all susceptible to manipulation
the sweet talk of agents
the foreign element takes root so easily
the duck-tailed youth
suspicious and sullen
the Mexican who left his trace the night before
Jose Dias on the front page
Leyvas who bears the shame
the guilty one
subjected to the facts
the fight outside a club
the boy who crossed the allotted space
the sanctity of a barrio
venturing forth
stupid in his English
swaggering down the street
ballooning pants and ankles pegged
his LA cool
his stoic moves on Central Avenue
did our elders not tell us to keep the spot dug for us
the table prepared
the time allotted
these provocations take hold so easily
now the sailors flowing over the banks
hundreds of cars and taxis
thousands from Main Street to Sunset
straight out of bootcamp
combing the haunts of pachucos
desperate to make the cut
remove the thorn
the offense that poisons
the rotten flesh festering silently
we gut our houses
destroy our pictures

dishes and artifacts
pull every root
the directive takes hold
rounded up
herded to the swamplands of Arkansas
the deserts of California

a neighborhood burns
smoke rises
limb separates from limb
eyes withdraw
smolder in silent places
inside us a landscape
never seen or touched by others
drawn to this corner or that corner
carried across the city
swallowed by the hills
Chapule turns to Pearl
Eternidad to Broadway

my head is smooth inside
dark and unsullied
no flesh to caress
no tentacles to reach for light
only the cold interior
dignified
unseen
silent
outside the sun shifts
a trail of color on a cloud
a robin at dawn
I look for faceless men
a parade of zoot suiters
the march of enemies in camps or a picture in a textbook
indexed and illustrated
to rise or sleep

spare my feet a journey
or seek the forgotten
waiting for time
to die once again or inhabit the cold gazes of passersby
petitions and sacraments
the incense of a single voice
a boy in the arms of his mother
a surgery gone well or badly
the birth of an infant in a day or two
a body eaten up with disease
it is too easy to speak
it is too difficult to learn these other paths
but we are blessed
the regular precautions still make room
the mathematical poise of physicians
measured skulls
knife opened wounds
carried forward by the inhuman instruments in our pockets

I depart
I exit
I stretch my skin
emerge from a womb of sleep
ease my way into the morning
underneath veins sink and rise
my heart shifts
innumerable hooks search bone
I set my body out for the feeding
saddled with streams of conversation
skin shot through with chatter
somewhere in the brain cells lodged take shape like art
the smallest of brush strokes builds a world
the light gathers arms and legs
put together
a phrase is a miracle passed with regret
I string words together

count out the conversations
unintelligible gestures of a language I cannot understand
the sun's mangy rays break loose
then freeze
my feet catch pavement
yellow brick
steel barred windows
skeletal trees
monumental sidewalks left or right
it makes no difference
the gait is impenetrable
the purpose the same
to meet the light
take hold of the coming day
I am the man with skin stretched
between eye and mouth
neither evening nor dawn
nothing alters
turns to shade or burns
the sun rises but there is no path
the silent moon
the murderous light
the silent moon
turn and shift
I am nothing
I am everything

I no longer remember the smell of blood
an animal giving birth at midnight is a wild curiosity
buried then raised in the brain
the insects we pick from amber
the trace of foreign habits in the eye of laboratory glass
in the confines of fabricated light
here are the Tongva and the council tree
made a state park for a Sunday outing
here are some bones in tar

here the people we drove to the East side of the river
and the stories we tell
and the films that explain the course of a day in their lives
destined as they are to live in the folds of our bodies
the corners of our mouths
here the soft hands we dug into the earth
the skin we grafted to the rocks of fields
the arms of trees
here the volcanic skin that formed in the earth's cool passing
the insects that floundered in bleeding trees
the marrow we cut from bone
all this survives a centuries worth of human predicament
a museum parade or geographical embarrassment
there are various places to hide
there are empty libraries to house stories of Yankee armies
there are cemeteries to bury our children
there are homes to house old women who remember the night
the sailors flowed across the river in search of zoot suiters

Chapter 2
Noon

she ran like a mad woman across the lawn
medusa hair caught in the wind
wild beasts
inhuman brutes chasing her down
she screamed when you caught her
all day you played with your sister like this
you were the king of a distant country or a
simple mechanic
you invited her for tea
you sipped air
chatted like old women
one day after the rain she took to the back yard
she discovered the enchantment of mud
sun baked patterns drying on the ground
ready for the taking
she pealed them off
displayed them
flung them toward the sky
then wet them again with a hose
the patterns disbanded into the soil
consumed by the earth
at dusk you showed her how to cut a mango
the juice ran down your cheeks
you ate till you were full

you carried her home
the clouds playing with her
covering then unveiling
covering again
through the corridors to the room
where you put her to sleep
and held her
and closed the curtains to keep her from the sun

Mother
I measured your heartbeat
told you where to step
I buried your feet in concrete
dammed the flow
you reached for the water deep below
in your ignorance
you forgot the hour at hand
the instruments in your pocket
the map in your head
you lived by the necessary things
the body's molecular requirements
the search for a field or a factory
thrust to barrios
supervised as children are supervised
no longer a Guatemalan woman
an elder in the village
a lover
a mother
I have seen Diego Rivera's mural on Sunset and Olivera
Dulles and Armas
shake hands among bodies and bananas
Eisenhower adorns a bomb
America Tropical mural
tasteless and grotesque
a sunburned landscape
a Guatemalan pyramid

coiled serpent trees
broken steles and stone from the temple
a large central figure
a Mexican Indian crucified on a double cross
perched on top
an American eagle
on the right side a pair of sharpshooters
aiming straight for it
how surprised they were these city bureaucrats
this muralist Siqueiros

> *he's political after all*

what would you have me paint he said

> *a continent of happy men*
> *surrounded by palms and parrots*
> *where fruit voluntarily detaches*
> *falls into the mouths of happy mortals*

come
they said

> *we will collect the remains*
> *wash ourselves*
> *we will cover his naked body*
> *we will comb his hair*

in the corner of the mural
the river begins to flow
the currents draw near
from village to village
the wind brushes against us
only the lightest touch and we fall
our bodies are too soft
too defenseless
the water rises

it carries us away
beyond this village to another nameless village
from El Infierno
through Quiché and Huehuetenango
from village to village
the Kaibiles come
trained in the killing of animals
they eat them raw
they drink their blood
through Chimaltenango
Alta and Baja Verapaz
have you seen them
heeded their warning
the birds scatter in the field
the curtains shift
the first shot breaks our sleep
through the windows
the silent house
the footsteps
through the curtains
merciless
into our dreams
the last conversation
the man and the women embraced in love
the child who stands by the window
or sleeps in her bed
we must not eat now
we must not make love now
the child must not stand by the window
or sleep in her bed
our hearts must not beat
we must hold the last breath
before the last breath
the sacred meal
the final embrace
                    the air is cold

Sky Gods and Chaos Monsters

the dogs are silent
our footsteps sound on the floor

come
look
your sister is sleeping

I never kissed her forehead
I never saw her
laid to rest
tell me to mourn
command me
but I can't
only the old repetitions keep faith
tears dry into skin
the nerves no longer connect
there is no grave
I have nothing to say
I do not hate war or love it
I do not burn candles in memorial or seek her face again
there are men who take hold of their last possession
burn bone
carve tongue
there are women who sing their mourning songs
they cut the silence
they sing of death and hurt with love
but why should we raise up our voices
floundering on forgotten trails
drunk with love
drunk with hate
I read my poems Mother
I see how they turn dirty in the morning
cast into another world with different rules
they turn with the shadows and the light outside
words are worn habits
there are no poems for children who die in their seventh year

men with cut off limbs
oh my love
you want me to build alters
silent wakes
funeral gatherings in church basements
this is what you seek
but there is no memory
only a poem
only the shape of sound
the color of meaning
I have long since stopped the search
called off the dogs
gotten married
gotten divorced
buckled up
I am the man with skin stretched
between eye and mouth
neither evening nor dawn
nothing alters
turns to shade or burns
the sun rises but there is no path
the silent moon
the murderous light
the silent moon
turn and shift
oh Guatemala
what became of you
oh primitive love
primitive hate
oh resentful gaze
abandon all your hate
abandon all your love
calculate every step
the earth is ours for the taking

strong to the point of tears

sharp as a knife
quiet and terrible
the eagle shoots and cries
the eagle cuts with tears
cuts himself with every extraction
hurts with every hurt inflicted
oh Zacapa
oh Panzos
oh Rabinal
all is tragedy
glorious and cruel

the civilized man
suffers the wounds he exacts
glorious and cruel
he pities the terror unleashed
triumphs in swift penitence
takes solace in the drawing room
with whip on back and broken skin
the smell of flesh is his perfume
blood his salve
he is a beast of prey
he is the prey
eagle and pregnant hare
he drives the hunt
he lays himself on the alter
delicate hand
clenched fist
cool and cruel
god and beast
suspended between wound and scab
the civilized man makes shape of hunger
vision of blood
he subdues the horror
lets it breathe again
lets the terror flow

through the measured artery
he hangs himself on a mathematical cross
solves every nail to perfection
calculates and calibrates
plots the next move
precious and fragile
stretched to heaven
graceful only in return
privileged with human prescience
sweet justice
glorious tragedy
come close
be noble
measure your love
measure your hate
fill the stage
carry the sound
act the part
the noble thespian
kills but kills with tears
kills but cuts himself in sorrow
glorious tragedy
war is art
art is suffering
let the suffering fuel your step
unleash the terror
subdue it
let the bile flow
dam it
tie your ankles and your wrists
secure the ropes
round the axles
turn the poles
dislocate the joints
stretch the god
stretch the monster

oh god of guilt
oh glorious suffering
we love you
we praise you
we worship you

the shape of a hill
remains a hill
an arch remains an arch against the sun
Royce's measured canopies
coffered ceilings
reach for the heavens
then return
graceful only in return
the brain calculates and calibrates
plots the next move
keeps watch
precious and fragile
outside the rabid strands of sunlight wear us down
wind eats soil
fields of dust stretch for miles
the markets fail in New York
inside we take paint to canvas
run our fingers against the cold walls
bricks red with consolation
cornered by our very own creation
limited by the lines we draw
we trace the edge of our concern
master each lombard shape
the dampened light of St. Sepolcro
San Ambrogios' human figure
the solid pathways keep faith
the Quads rectangular precautions
the soft-footed steps and watered grass rise from the reservoir
every measurement draws a new frontier
there are too many thoughts scattered in our heads

we must take stock
cut and preserve
protect the human race
during these worst of days
keep watch of foreign armies
the zoot suiter lost on the boulevard
the Armenian terrorist hiding in the trees
all who stray too far
below Powell's twin towers
in the solace of candlelight
cafes thick with smoke and flirt
the poet sits with pen in hand
the delicate hand
the clenched fist
clamoring for war
clamoring for peace
cool and cruel
he weighs our options in Royce and Haines
in the halls of Kinsey the historian warns of anarchists in Spain
the theologian solves the Great Mystery
in his mind
the psychologist says
we are not animals
we are animals
we are gods
we are beasts
in Rodin's garden
look mother
a rot iron eagle
headless atop a nameless monster
between his legs
spread apart
a screaming gargoyle
ready for the taking
the artist proclaims
I know you too well

you are that eagle god
you are that wretched beast
you are the vile mask
you are the poet who awakens from the horror
who calls the dream a nightmare
shudders
divides and conquers
reclaims the watchful post again
cornered in musty studios
the eagle emerges
in the hot hour of creation
the artist shapes the solid form
leaves a rubble of stone
a grave of dreams
now soiled with rain
the plaything of thieves
students branding love in stone
shape and stance turn cold
in the eyes of the wisest
the bespeckled critic squints
measures and nods
the juice that ran the joints
the wild eye
frozen in betrayal
deep below
bile governs the comings and goings
drives the beat
far above
the eagle gathers the future
sets the laws for generations to come
the eagle subdues all vengeance
expels every anarchist
every soiled thought festering in the darkness
sharp as a knife
quiet and terrible
the eagle shoots and cries

bleeds and heals
heals and bleeds
throws the spear
confesses in a mirror
oh glorious suffering
oh glorious pain
oh meaningless meaning
graceful arch
graceful love
graceful hate
oh god of guilt
we love you
we praise you
we worship you

look Mother
below Powell's watch towers
the savage children you love so much
April 26
down Sunset
arm in arm
the vile march
through Little Armenia
the insurgents
their skulls on fire
their blood-filled eyes
their primitive love
their primitive hate
their savage love
boiling over with hate

My son
see below
at the bottom of the hill
a row of skeleton houses

a deserted ghost town
a father cries
sprinkles red cherries on a tombstone to feed
the spirit of his children
he reaches for a weed in the overgrown
graveyard

> *they plucked my children*
> *like flowers*
>
> *may I go blind*
> *if you do not take vengeance*

the boy awakens
to the sound of footsteps outside
the voices of men through the window
he joins the caravan along the Euphrates
across desserts and over mountains
past the empty villages
the swollen bodies
the caverns they used for the burnings
past the spot where they fired
where the gendarmes pulled the boy's sister out
raped her
struck his brother
cracked open his skull
through the village
the smoldering rubble
through the fields
where they buried their jewelry
across the Tigris
legs caught in the rapids
donkeys crushed by the refrigerators
on their backs

the story repeats itself
behind the boy
the village still burns

Noon

ash catches current
high above
a Sikorsky Black Hawk beats the air
in search of PKK
the methods are crude
mark the village
all terrorist
then leave it in rubble

make no mistake
all who do not protect the village
are terrorists

the boy screams but it is the last time he'll
scream like this
he cries but never again like this again
fear passes through his hands

> *Talaat is here*
> *and yet you do not seem concerned*
>
> *you are no longer my son*
> *come close Talaat*
>
> *may I go blind*
> *if you do not take vengeance*
>
> *I have killed a man*
> *but I am not a murder*
>
> *so it must be*
> *should your Father's corpse visit you*
> *speak and exhort you*

holy Aratat
holy Sun
the boy who sleeps like a lamb
awakens
to the fortress dance
spinning in circles
every single animal

roused
he leaps and runs
springs out for the hunt
merciless
he unleashes the ambush

> *ag ag ag*

the boy shields his eyes
as the sun rises on every hidden mystery
the terror in his heart exposed
below him
a ravaged herd of cattle
a trail of blood
limb torn from limb
we should have cast the iron net
but we woke him instead
innocent and cruel
ignorant in his misery
now he stands with head in hand
wild and lost
bloody face in the mirror
primitive love
primitive hate
savage love
boiling over with hate

> *father*
> *state*
> *teachers rise up*
> *the new generation will be your creation*

they who cannot walk properly
or read the language of our intellectual achievements
they who squat on sidewalks
live by the generosity in our hearts
crass and hungry
the gargoyle screams
his savagery is limitless

the zoot suiter is bile
the Armenian terrorist is bile
the civilized killer
governs the bile in himself
he is worthy to govern the bile on the street
primitive love
primitive hate
savage love
boiling over with hate
the eagle puts it all to sleep
oh men of mercy
we praise you
we worship you

one day the child will pity your frailty
Mother
hour upon hour
counting out the minutes
he lives for another day
after this day
he waits
grows tired and old
on his death bed
with the last gasp
the same devoted servant
the terrorist child
cannot contain the jealous charge
full up with bile
he detonates in the noon hour sun
with dumb enthusiasm
he holds the pistol
the pistol snaps
makes the extraction
removes the festering element
not in the shadows
or along the side-streets

or in the back alley
but in the light of day
do not pity the boy
he is a man
through the streets
down Sunset
arm in arm
the vile march
through Little Armenia
April 26
the raspy voice
bloody voice
the only pure voice
the only music he will ever sing
hear him prophesy in the empty coffeeshop
see him wound the passersby
the innocent poet
the stupid children
the family and the dog
their Sunday noon prance
he opens the scab
shames them all
foils the innocent facade
strips the paint and all the moorings
do not pity him
he knows the punishment to come
the story repeats itself
the Blackhawk still hovers
the village still burns
the hot breath of vengeance lingers
behind each child
the daughters of darkness rise up
no one will escape the gathering sorrow
the secluded spot in the distant field grows old
the ballot falls
the urn of blood commands

it is a hard heart he put in our breast Hampig
justice commando man
a savage breed from a savage father
you conquered our inhibitions
your cruelty made us cruel
the undiluted substance
the torrent in our body
the merciless wind
you unleashed it all
I have heard their whispers
one by one
down Sunset
across the river
through Little Armenia
these very same streets
all susceptible to manipulation
the sweet talk of foreign agents
across the river
again and again
animal skin man
greaser man
with flowing hair
swaggering down the street
coming to rob us cold
bleed us
feed us with their trash
take our girls
hold up in ghettos
living on handouts
living because we stood them up straight
across the river
ridiculous in their suits
long with envy
floundering about
getting knocked down knocked up
shot to pieces

we comforted Hampig at the last hour
we closed his eyes
left him on the street
broken-legged and lost
the last act of justice is the purifying hand
weak and dumb
in the drunken hour
the savage walks to his death at Clear Lake
the intoxicated brain mercifully put to sleep
the terrorist child
justly denied
that last drop of avarice
come close breathe hard
trembling earth
blessed famine and disease
the work of gunships is done
the deed accomplished
these cruelties were written long before
now set the suffering free
let them take their last breath
take root again in the coldest surface
if they can
give them room again
one last chance to prove there's a god beating inside
waiting for release
we who are more merciful
than the merciful
civilized killers
plow the soil
cast your net on all the beasts
level all the hills
we who are more merciful
than the merciful
we do not celebrate life and happiness
our justice is unrelenting
oh men of mercy

Noon

set the suffering free

you take things too far Mother
your impropriety poisons us all
there are men who do not deserve your glance
the warmth in your hand
a single hello
there was a time when poets built languages that made us breathe
differently
go to war differently
they filled air with spit
turned night to verse and when we awoke in the morning
we'd know how to move properly
our voices and our hands calling out the beat again
these songs are still on our lips
the stroke that rids our city of river banks and failing bridges
makes shape of blossoms ready for the taking
I have seen the light alter the contour of a single day
the noon-day sun in Rodin's garden take hold of the earth
burn dew to mist
if you would let me speak with the assurance of paved rivers
with the calm of conquered bulls
I would show you the irrefutable faces of exploit and
accomplishment
the crease and pattern of skin consumed by the sun
I would speak of my father's father
the ancestors who lent us name and place
who dug the soil around our feet
fashioned a home from mud
you would know of these facts formed under this sky
the knowledge held in hand
I would tell of a few mud huts by the river
a dirt path destined for a cow pasture
linked to wagon trails
stretching 24 miles to their drowning

how we moved further and further through the hills to find our
shelter
how we came for silence and spiritual meetings
built polo fields
retired to our homes
protected from lesser sorts by sycamore groves
then Sunset Boulevard through the hills
a terrible vain from Perishing Square to the ocean
100 teams of horses
gouging out the hills
crumbling banks saved only by mural walls
east to west
pushing towards the edge
we stood our ground on the cliffs
in the last hour
our voices and our hands calling out the beat
Great Mystery too far to reach
we offer you thanks
indifferent stars
we give you thanks
you sowed your seed and left the soil to us
you let us suffer
create a new earth and another after that
the birthday of a new world is at hand
flood upon flood
merciful flood
merciful concrete
New Jerusalem
City on Hill
Great Mystery
we give you thanks
oh Jerusalem
oh Spirit of Amalek
our justice is unrelenting
we who are more merciful than the merciful

the kid who burns his brains
the murderer and the victim
the scum who beats his wife
the wife beaten to a pulp
every single one bears down on you Mother
there is misery enough to go around
the half dead and half alive in Boyle Heights
the slothful living in forgotten apartments
trailers and city streets
go shake Hampig's hand
invite him inside
from the highway and the side streets
invite them all
this is your privilege
let them stare you in the face
inspect every inch
they will laugh at you
they will see nothing but the shell of love
a dismantled body on the floor where they dropped it
across the bridge
they come
ready to steal that last drop of love
waiting for you
while you eat your supper
at the supper table
suckling at your breasts
while you take your rest with your family
in the family room
perched in the corner
while you sleep on your bed
in the bedroom
the candle on the supper table shifts in the breeze
a crack in the window
the wick smolders
the bitter nostril
the stinging eye

the solution is always the same
cower in fear
or bring out the scalpel
sever the heart
or detonate
what now
will you go or stay
go to Leyvas and kiss him on the mouth
we are not alike
I am a civilized man
I suffer the wounds I exact
glorious and cruel
I pity the terror unleashed
all is tragedy
whip on back
broken skin
the kid who burns his brains
the murderer and the victim
the scum who beats his wife
the wife beaten to a pulp
I severed it all
I abandoned it all to the deep
loving Mother
shameless Mother
the earth is ours

laugh if you will Mother
stuck on a Casbah mural wall
chipped and forgotten
lost and useless
you who haven't felt a muscle since that first coat of paint
from time to time
a strand of air
at the outer edge
a lilac breeze
a drop of rain

on your face
you can almost feel it
the colors hold fast
purple remains purple
blue remains blue
solid sky
solid earth
the cars pass
children play beneath you
a saint opens his mouth and prays to you
you have lived at Sunset and Hyperion too long
caught in our imagination
we prayed to you
lectured on you
debated you in the seminary cafe
we heard your name called at our city's birth
the name escapes with ease
carried with a flourish
Mother Mary
stuck on a mural wall
chipped and forgotten
take leave
suffer the empty street
touch ground again
let the pavement settle
let the light shine in your eyes
watch closely
an Arabic man and a French women begin to dance
the drift of Rai and coffee
the hovering melisma
the American pulse
the Ber Ber beat
what would you prefer
English Breakfast or Renee's Chai
Darjeeling or Japanese Green
a pita and hummus

quiche or camembert baguette
an empanada or prosciutto
in the back
Turkish towels
vetements and Indian silk
the palate is swift and crude
the colors swallow
brusque green
brick red
resolute blue
mercifully
the gentrified playground
protects us
loves us
it cannot hate
it neither loves nor hates
oh sweet void
oh calculated cruelty
Mother Mary
stuck on a mural wall
chipped and forgotten
lost and useless

       I met a man here once
       in the summer of '68
       his name was Cesar Chavez
       he came marching one day
       he stopped the hungry crowd
       and lingered by the sunlit wall
       the day before we'd made our way down to the
       jail
       canned food and clothes in our trunk for the
       grape harvesters
       we hurried off to the picket-line
       paraded in the dust outside Council Chambers
       inside our man locked up

Noon

beaten by a scab
we dodged stones and spit
the curses of young men
gunning past us in old pickups

  agitator
  commie
  red

but we got him
I remember how we celebrated
Cesar greeting us
I remember how he stepped forward
he touched me
so small and quiet

his words were a salve
our embrace a prayer
I remember the marches down Sunset
those first days
the coffee house conversations
the conceptual commotion
the preserved state of devotion
readings by candlelight
the Thursday evening
coming and going
rooms thick with steam and flirt
resistance
laughter
worship
I was there at the last march
surrounded by hundreds of farm workers and
their families
it was dangerous this sight
this coffin
the polished body
threatening to hemorrhage

to speak again at any moment
on the dais
a troupe of dancers
spinning in circles
I held them all in my arms
Indians
Latinos
White
Black
like those first days
then the rhythmic clapping rising in the night

> *Si se puede*
> *Viva Cesar Chavez*
> *Viva la unión*

a priest singing

> *Resucito resucito*

the Indians dancers in counterpoint

> *Chavez is made from corn*
> *his soul is made of corn*

the mourners moving closer

> *Cesar I miss you*
> *I've missed you for a long time*

the songs prevailed
for a time
then the despotic days at Tehachapis
the vulgar interruption
seeps in
poisons the mind
shall I tell tales of a tyrant
or an angel
shall I tell you of his sour voice over the phone
the first time he called me Mister instead of Brother
his rehab facility

hold up in a mountain compound
crazy talk of young upstarts
purges to cleanse the movement
the spirit of Cesar is frail
it will not survive
Mother
your child will eat his young
unleash the juice stored inside
the delicate heart
the feeble body cannot defend the civilized cause
build the solid thing
your child loved too much
his love turned to hate
his love boiled over
he gathered all the vengeance
unleashed it all
it is ages since the first fast
since the first prayer
the beggar on the corner
the leper once kissed
his love is too forceful for lullabies
he moves by the seething blood inside his body
the swollen body
expanding and contracting
weaving the perfect plan
for the killing
ferocious simplicity
the deeds that live
because he gives them life
the knife he hides sits in pocket
shifty and unexpected
he searches for the solid thing
the diagnosis
the evil thing
the thing that sticks to hand
carves teeth

stacks bones
he is merciless
because he is merciless
restless because he is restless
he cannot hold his children
because he cannot hold his children
dangling
suspended in climax
the violent calm
before the violent deed
he lives for a day
lives for a season
passes with the season
returns
this curse
this prophetic skill
the attentive eye
there is nothing to write
there is no verse
it is cowardly to sit eloquently in the cafe corner
to sit in the shadows
while the ordinary hero lives the ordinary day
there are no poems for your terrorist child
there is no breath to speak
when the shadows grow long and his love expires
with nothing more to sing
there is only blood under his fingernails
there is no dignity
in dying
he is too wise
too ignorant
he flew too far
with heavy feet and useless mind
an accident
a mutation
a curse

the plaything of waves
oh Spirit of Amalek
lost on the shore
caught in the sand
waiting for the spear
Great Mystery
save us from this pestilence
punish us
Mother Mary
your poems retreat in the light
soiled by the sun
beyond the custody of eloquence
your children speak your name
but there is no hill high enough
historical enough
beautiful enough
to hide their faces from the sun
Mother Mary
who kissed you
at whose feet did you fall
who held you in that last hour
before your last hour
you who fell in love
starved yourself in love
grew in hate
kissed the leper
again and again
lived on nothing
Mother
I know better
the sun foils every plan
the civilized man measures every drop of love
he raises himself from the dead
tames the beast
lets the terror flow
through the measured artery

he owns every phrase
calculates every knife stroke
cuts with precision
carves bone
stacks them all in order
the solid thing
the calibrated brain
the civilized cause
loving Mother
shameless Mother
oh Spirit of Amalek
primitive love
primitive hate
with one turn
your children turned desperate
ate their young
unleashed the juice stored inside
the savage torrent
black blood boiling
trembling earth
sunken beast
merciful spear
oh Jerusalem come quickly
end the suffering
purify the world of love
and hate
measure every heartbeat
tell us where to step
bury our feet in concrete
dam the flow
Great Mystery
we will never reach for the water deep below
we will never forget the hour at hand
the instruments in our pockets
the maps in our heads
Great Mystery too far to reach

we offer you thanks
indifferent stars
we give you thanks
Great Mystery
draw the blade
let these tongues of light scatter
let the builders thrive
let the parasites fail
oh god of guilt
we love you
we praise you
we worship you

Chapter 3
Dusk

on the sidewalk an LA Times scattered
the business page flaps in the breeze
this morning while the sun rose and the markets were high
imperial declarations
solemn proclamations
drove the beat
now men return home to torture their cats
make something resonate in the dark
the faithful edge of our survival
broken by the daily retreat to lesser worlds
impotent conclusions
past the Marlboro man and fiberglass showgirl
with twirled stripes and silver dollar toe
inflamed above me
a bright-eyed sign
a billboard in the night
a brassy Pepsi songstress with open stance and aromatic
shoulders
a rivulet of hair rests on her collarbone
she is a single flame frail against the darkness
I resurrect myself
one more night
one more field to plow
settlement to conquer

Dusk

a soap bubble
a game at dusk

doux présent du présent

I hold every second
squeeze
suffocate
the final minute
the last goodnight
the last call of the robin
before the sun's descent
before the skeleton tree
the final minute
before the final minute
a voyage to west
Pepsi girl in hand
past angular houses
a tide of white flowing down burnt slopes to Sunset
the Marmont
a fairy dream
slips past us down the hill
silently through the mud
grab hold Pepsi girl
you are not dead yet
turn up the volume
let the street grow louder
the billboards taller
fall in line
past the gawking cruisers
the parade of cars
the reverential train
past the strutters and the players
the heroic breasts and molecular faces
through the House of Blues
claim your refuge in Pucks

the solemn space for the weary traveler
pastel perfect with a dose of sunlight
the angular sanity
a slip of the hand
covered with a napkin
the private gaze
the motion of a finger
a turn of phrase
all is crowded solitude
every line rehearsed in bathroom mirrors
Pepsi girl
stay silent while I speak
do not look
do not dismiss
the proper tranquility of my habits
the formal certainty of mode and practice
the decorum of trivial things
the restaurant that bears its meaning in silver wear
the witticism that fills silence
do not speak child
hold every second
the persistence of your words
the speech that makes for silence
in voice and hand
in the manner your fingers meet skin
the breath you lend forgotten children
discard it all
do not speak child
hold every second
squeeze
suffocate
the last goodnight
the last call of the robin
the final minute
before the final minute

Dusk

an unexpected noise

a man much more drunk than us
bursts through the door
we turn our heads
in tandem

> the world is ending
> the world is ending

my love
we have one thing left

one thing to hold

> doux présent du présent

the moment
before the last moment
do not fear
there are too many thoughts scattered in our heads
we must take stock
cut and preserve
protect the human race
during these worst of days
keep watch of foreign armies
the zoot suiter lost on the boulevard
the Armenian terrorist hiding in the trees
all who stray too far
these hills still invite themselves beneath our skin
make space for us by the hearth
lull us to better places
we who know the value of these prizes
the dark sheen of polished classics
the dark wood of furniture
the open places of living room and nook
the rest we deserve from the knowledge of hate and gangs in
battle
foreign places made desolate by war
this is all in keeping

my love
we no longer share our fate with creatures run mad by fear
cursed with trembling skin
wild scent
the hunt for a mate in spring
move with me
follow the beat
hold my hand
down Sunset
the last hour is now
the last stand
the last moment
before the last moment
we are not dead yet

fill the empty space
take your stand at Mondrian and Standard
all is empty
ready for the taking
nothing breathes here
nothing takes air
nothing moves
lives or dies
a piece of glamour
a touch of whimsy
here or there
Alice in Wonderland doors
thirty foot mahogany
a bar of light
through the skull
an elevator bank in a glowing cube
onward to the rumpus room
the conversation pit
the half nude model napping in the fish tank
awful green
fragments

Dusk

awful offense
be offended if you must
take the bait
drama queen
make your scene in the naughty lobby
behold a women with breasts to bear
on a shimmering wall
scream at this if you must
learn the game
pick a corner
collect the remains
scoff at the hipsters lounging on pillows
the performance artist mowing the electric blue Astro Turf
salvage the pieces
from another time
a shag carpet
the chrome Arco lamps
the egg-shaped chairs
love it all
the way you loved it yesterday

doux présent du présent

the evening remains
a sculpture
a painting
a song to conquer ears
fashion tears
to balance a compliment and a coffee
in perfect alignment
to win an audience over dessert
to force the eyes of strangers
I'll wear you around my neck
or on my fingers
under the lights
I'll entangle you in my eyes

pick your face apart
the game is hard
you armless creature
ready to bear my complicated body
I've filled my storehouse with skin and bones
you are the last
before the last
let your body unfold
let the soiled light sweep you clean
learn the swagger and the boast
let the mutilated bass pound the floor
the methodical dance
the surgical pronouncements
the biological requirements
dive with me
let your body fall in line
let the pieces fall
collect them
let them fall again
fall and collect
collect and fall
the night is cadaverous
eyeless
useful only for copulation
you goddess with bronze skin and fleshy thighs
let me dig the soil around your feet
fill your empty heart
before the day is done
sweet women
one last time
somewhere
someplace
Pepsi goddess
the last hour is now
the last stand
the present moment

before the final moment
you are not dead yet
hold on
squeeze
hold
squeeze
you will not inherit the earth
every accomplishment or failure
each square tilled or partitioned by quarrel
or molded to satisfaction
you will inherent nothing
dawn after dawn
glorious mind
helpless mind
sweet concrete river my love

Chapter 4
Night

I have swallowed and all is gone
conversations warm in the mouth
deliberations zealous and grave
retreat to private hold-outs
cloistered shelters
the embrace of human sound
sanguine proclamations
thick with face and eye
evaporate in the shifting light
in every corner of the hills
a light burns
a family gathers
conversations wrapped in darkness
secrets divulged
somewhere a mother and a child
caught in each other's arms
breathe the same air
finish each other's sentences
you will accuse me
you will say
I am envious
but I don't suffer the petty goings on
the purple moods
the sad embrace of men and women in love

there's a common space shared by the blessed
tied to each other's veins
they suffer their madness
repeat themselves
shall I give her flowers
shall I touch her on the shoulder
or kiss her on the neck
shall I breathe on her
or will she fall apart
these shoes we must remove
these prayers we must pray
this tenderness that brings into our arms
the recollection of days
discarded in the waste of ordinary living and dying
these places invite too much
call too forcefully
there's a plague of hair on our backs
up our noses
tied down
connected to the mouths and eyes of others
the required glance
the hands we must touch
the dirty secrets
the dirty course of a day
I sever each strand
I cut out my tongue
I search the night for some saving indifference
a mirror to pick my zits
some song
some show
some trifle
some light in the eyes
some beat to drive my body from this place
to speak it all away
the blue lights flickers
fastens the last portion of evening

empties itself for my sake
pundit banter
eager talk of actors in marital disarray
the mischief of politicians in Washington
every detail swallows me
draws me further into the dark

as you crossed the bridge
my child
you held the Pepsi girl
she pulled away from your drunken grasp

then fell on the cement

you woke from the dream

and you took her home
you begged for forgiveness
why did you look her in the eyes
in the doorway
the final glace
before the final glance

did you see the patterned light
in her eyes
did you hold her heart in your hands

you yearned for her once

but you forgot her

my son
she is not the billboard goodness on Sunset
or the girl on the corner in your dreams
you tried to eat the last morsel

Night

but you did not destroy her
or make her
you cannot wear her on your fingers
she cannot dig your grave
she will return to the land
build a house by a creek and a hollow of sycamores
she will yearn and mourn and yearn again
each and every evening
she will dance with her lover by the widow
two in one
one in two

in your head
in your father's
father's
head
she rises from the sand
breathes fire into the wind
she wipes the salt from her skin
the deluded thought breaks your legs
you stumble
you shoot the first arrow and she sinks into the sea
you build the heavens and the earth from her carcass
from birth a wilderness in your dreams
you governed the pace and execution
shaped her
in your dreams
filled the hollow heart
in your dreams
the undiluted substance
the torrent in her body
the merciless wind

Mother Mary
your accusations fail

my son
you cannot create
you cannot destroy
at dawn
each and every blood trail
sinew and limb
takes shape
shapes yearning for shape
atoms tuned to atoms
the everlasting bird song spins in her ears
there is a seed inside her heart
the seed yearns for the sun
for the dark below your feet
the everlasting tree sprouts
words purple with love rise in the light
between the willows and the cottonwoods
roots grow into the ground
fed by streams far below
the tree grows tall and populates the soil
encircles the globe
at dusk it falls to ground and sinks into the earth
it emerges at dawn again
it reaches for the sun
a word sprouts
then another
another and another
word paired with word
four in one
one in four
harmony in love melody
melody in love with harmony
before the sun's descent
before the skeleton tree
day after day

Night

in the final minute
before the final minute
I speak to her again
I dry my tears and hold her in my arms
the air escapes her lungs
she sheds her skin and with the last breath

sees my face

my child
you fumbled the dance
you broke the movements
Cesar hid from your gaze and set you free
I held you both once at Hyperion and Sunset
I shielded your eyes
as the sun rose on every hidden mystery
I sang to you
swaying to the beat
the music swirled in your ears
faster and faster
until you rose
spinning in circles
the yearning in your heart exposed
faster and faster
until you leapt and ran through the streets

in your head
in your father's head
the beast keeps pace
falls in step
down Sunset
arm in arm
through Little Armenia
the ghost town child
hides in the grass
behind him

the Blackhawk hovers
the hot breath of vengeance on his neck
behind each child
in your dreams
you build a fence
draw the measurements
calculate all the angles
you cut stone from earth
columns rise
higher and higher
until the day of vengeance
dissolves every watch tower
and your wooden roofs turn to ash
with face open to the heavens
you flee the beast
cover your body with leaves and animal fur
to deceive your father
defy his call
day after day
your eyes shoot arrows
day after day
you survive on the edge of wild nights
between sleep and sleep
your blood stumbles through your body

                    Mother Mary
                    your accusations fail

the beast is your only friend
a mouth to starve
a mouth to feed
the juice inside your body
the kid who burns his brains
the murderer and the victim
the scum who beats his wife

the wife beaten to a pulp
the half dead and half alive in Boyle Heights
men and women living in forgotten apartments
trailers and city streets
from birth a wilderness in your dreams
you governed the pace and execution
you built an eagle god
you built a wretched beast
you joined them in one
master and slave
you watched the master fail
two in one
one in two
you unleashed it all
you caught the last seed before it fell to ground
before it took root
before it found the sun
before it populated the soil
you said
the child will never yearn and mourn again
never dance with his lover by the widow
the child is a wild space hungering for a name
an empty page
a mouth begging for blood
your enemy is a dream
you are a dream in your enemy's head
a dream of dreams
the wilderness in your head
becomes a wilderness
the empty page an empty page
the dream a concrete river
the terrorist child is your only friend
your savior
starve
feed
starve

feed
he is a gathering force
the summoning call
your will
your will to will
you are a dream in your master's head
a dream in your slave's head
a dream of dreams
do not mourn
do not cut
you cannot create
you cannot destroy

your heart still beats
you still breathe
the nerve endings still connect
but you forgot
you are the brother
you were
before they came
before the last game you played
through the dusty streets
past the sun-burnt buildings
the strands of heat in your nostrils
the cutting smells in your mouth
you are still the man
who carried your sister home
the clouds playing with her
covering then unveiling
covering again
through the corridors to the room
where you put her to sleep
held her
closed the curtains to keep her from the sun
though I cannot speak with you
I will follow you

Night

through the building I cleaned
through the corridors and numbered rooms
down the elevator shaft to the basement
through the wires and pipes
the silence of their hum
one day you will find what you seek
hidden from sight
behind a mop in a closet
a trail of soap left behind
by a pail of water
under cloth capillaries
trails weaved for dipping
submerged tentacles in a bucket
by a wall burned of blood
with hands and knees and fingers to the edge
in the darkest corner
you will see each face known since birth
each cherry tree
each street and lilac bush that had its place
on those ragged days
when your skin betrays your veins
when the things you hold come to pieces
between your fingers
a seed will sprout in your heart
in your enemy's heart

day after day
in the final minute
before the final minute
her feet sink into the mud
sun baked patterns dry on the ground
ready for the taking
she peals them off
displays them
flings them toward the sky
then wets them again with a hose

the patterns disband
consumed by the earth
at dusk she eats a mango
the juice runs down her cheeks
she eats till she is full
day after day
in the final minute
before the final minute
before the sun's descent
before the skeleton tree
I speak to her again
I dry my tears and hold her in my arms
the air escapes her lungs
and in the last moment
she sheds her skin
and with the last breath

sees my face

she is

a single note

a leaf on a branch

a strand of light

a trail of love

she is a bird yearning for her mate
the plaything of waves
trembling soil
sacred earth

my son
you are wise now

Night

wise as anyone who has learnt to grieve
take axe to pine
raise the Kotoomut pole
hang your mortuary baskets on the branches
remember her
the soil will take her memory
your children's children will forget her
but they will love and mourn and yearn again
they will remember the songs
the shape of each dance
the everlasting breath between note and note

somewhere walls are burnt
and smoke gives way like incense
the day of naming is a story kept in pocket
you will find it in the weaving room
or the wine presses above the mission
in the corners of the flour mill
under a fruit tree or a vine on the hills
where the earth endures uprooted trees
and open gashes breathe in the air

I am a god
I am a beast
I am a master
I am a slave
I am the war
suspended between scab and wound
namer and the named
creator and the creature

dominator and dominated
sky-god spectator and chaos monster

I am nothing

Mother
I am two

you will never understand
this is all I am
all I have
nothing more
I cut myself
with every extraction
hurt with every hurt inflicted
I am the drunkard on the edge of camp
in the shadows
out of reach
the one who sways
lurches
crumbles in the leaves
I am the one who falls asleep under the alders
the one who suffers in sleep with blood stained
leg and scattered mind
I am the vigilant skull
ensnared by the roots of trees
the one who scours the earth for heathen flesh
to collect the remains
I am the one who cuts the roots at dawn
with foot on the neck
and knife in hand
suspended between whip and spear
I cut
I bleed
I cut
I bleed
I gather the limbs
scatter them in the dust
hold
squeeze
squeeze

Night

hold

I am nothing
I am two
Mother

my child
listen

a seed in your heart searches for light
a prayer ascends

the Great Mystery
is a bird song without end
or beginning
in the beginning
in the end
day after day
the Great Mystery falls in love
falls for the dance
day after day
first heaven
then earth
dreadful Wiyot
blessed Chehooit
Tamit and Moar
Tobohar and Pabavit
first one
then two
then three
then four
the dance twirls and swells
day after day
the membrane of sleep tears at the edges
the sun scrapes the surfaces of stones

tongues of flame shake the night away
along the shore the Great Mystery takes air
the sun burns her breath
warms her skin
day after day
between body and bank
rock and shadow
she lands on the shore
rises from the sand
breathes fire into the wind
she wipes the salt from her skin and bellows for a mate
the call gathers her limbs
day after day
she finds her lover along the brook
she gazes at him and he calls her over
they dance in circles until sleep
two in one
one in two

you emerge
with the sun
with the unfolding sky
day after day
outside the hut
the Great Mystery gives birth
the currents of her womb
brush against your ears
her heartbeat counts out the rhythms
she holds you in the purifying steam and watches
as you break your swaddling clothes
she does not live in your dreams
she lives in the sea
she lives in the brook that runs through a forest of oaks
she lives along the hollow nearest the mission
she lives inside the soil
behind the wine presses above the mission

between the willows and the cottonwoods
she lives in the wild roses and grape-vines
where you cleared the hollow of every living thing
she sprouts in the sun
feeds the earth
she lines the furrows of the soil
her roots nourish your children and their children
atom tuned to atom
molecule tuned to molecule
she draws the patterns
between the exhaled breath and the inhaled breath
through your nostrils to the inner parts
she arrives and lives and dies and lives
taken in by soil
reborn in spring

she is the beast in the ocean
a rabbit fleeing north
she is the eagle hunter flying across the desert
she is the south-bound river now buried in concrete
four in one
one in four
she is a crow yearning for a mate
she is the mating ritual
a union of lovers
mother and father
seed and womb
earth and heaven
all things yearn for her
she yearns for all things
she is harmony in love with melody
melody in love with harmony
lover and beloved
yearning and yearned for
footprint and footpath
time-bound nomad and final destination

my child
nothing belongs to you
you are four in one
one in four
the Great Mystery
is neither seed nor womb
first breath nor last breath
sky nor earth
she does not live inside a poem
or in the book on your alter
all things live in her
nothing can contain her
your measurements and calculations hum in tune
motion paired with motion
yearning with yearning
your breath resonates
finds its way between note and note
your body vibrates
between limb and limb
your science is your art
your art is your science
knowledge is life
measurement a dance
the melody finds the chord
the Great Mystery unfolds
each and every blood trail
sinew and limb
takes shape
shapes yearning for shape
atoms tuned to atoms
the everlasting bird song spins
the seed in your father's enemy's heart
reaches for the sun
for the dark below your feet
the everlasting tree spouts

Night

words purple with love rise in the light
between the willows and the cottonwoods
roots grow deep into the ground
fed by streams far below
at dusk a tree falls to ground
sinks into the soil
then emerges at dawn again
inside your enemy's heart
inside your heart
a word sprouts
then another
another and another
word paired with word
four in one
one in four
harmony in love melody
melody in love with harmony
before the sun's descent
before the skeleton tree
in the final minute
before the final minute
I speak to you again
I dry my tears and hold you in my arms
the air escapes your lungs
and in the last moment
you shed your skin
and with the last breath

oh lover of earth and sky

you see my face

you are

a single note

a leaf on a branch

a strand of light

a trail of love

you is a bird yearning for his mate
the plaything of waves
trembling soil
sacred earth

my son
you are wise now
wise as anyone who has learnt to grieve
take axe to pine
raise the Kotoomut pole
hang your mortuary baskets
the soil will take your memory
your children's children will forget you

but they will love and mourn and yearn again

they will remember the songs

    the shape of each dance

        the everlasting breath between note and note

www.ingramcontent.com/pod-product-compliance
Lightning Source LLC
Chambersburg PA
CBHW072017170626
46813CB00005B/2172